POOF!

How to study spelling words:

1. Read a word.
2. Say the word out loud.
3. Try to remember all the letters in the word.
4. Try to write the word from memory.
5. Check to see if you were right.

Make your own spelling dictionary. Write down words you have trouble spelling, the meaning of the words and any trick you know that might help you remember how to spell the words.

Ms. Spell

by Ethan Long

Holiday House / New York

To all my teachers,
especially Mrs. Arcuri

Library of Congress Cataloging-in-Publication Data
Long, Ethan.
Ms. Spell / Ethan Long. — First Edition.
pages. cm.
ISBN 978-0-8234-3292-9 (hardcover)
1. English language—Orthography and spelling—Juvenile literature.
2. Vocabulary—Juvenile literature. 3. Children's poetry, American. I. Title.
PE1145.2.L66 2015
428.1—dc23
2014019145

That's okay. It is a common mistake. *There* sounds exactly like *their* and *they're*, but these three words all mean different things.

POOF!

Their father is a fireman.
They're going to the library.
There is a bug in my hair!

They're is a contraction that means "they are."

All three words begin with the letters TH.

The letter E at the end of *there* and *they're* is silent.

I want to spell *something*!
I want to spell *something*!

Breaking up long words into smaller words may help you remember spelling.
some + thing = something
some + time = sometime

Then spell *something*!
It's one of our spelling words!

S O M E T H I N G

"These TWO boys are crazy flying monkeys with laser beams shooting out their eyes!"
Oh boy. I have a bad feeling about this one.
Elephants red, hippos blue, I like monkeys; how about you?
There are **two** doughnuts left.
Mom took us **to** the zoo.
Cats have fur and dogs do **too**.

PEW! PEW!
THIS IS THE END, MY FRIENDS!
In fact, *friend* happens to be one of our spelling words! But there's no time for spelling now!
RUNNNNNNNNNNNN!
In the word *friend*, the letter *I* comes before the letter *E* and makes a short-*E* sound. But in words such as *neighbor* and *weigh*, the letter *E* comes before the letter *I* and makes the long-*A* sound.
The word **friend** ends in *end*.

Some Spelling Rules

1. *I* before *E* except after *C* or except when sounded like "ay," as in *neighbor* and *weigh*.

2. Silent *E* helps a vowel say its name. (When a word ends with a vowel followed by a consonant and then silent *E*, the vowel has a long sound. That's the difference between *bit* and *bite*, *cap* and *cape* and *car* and *care*.)

3. When two vowels go walking, the first one does the talking. (When there are two vowels in a row, the first usually has a long sound, and the second is silent. This is true in *wait* and *people*.